Curious George®
The Boat Show

YOUR TICKET TO MORE *Curious George*®

Download dozens of fun activities to help reinforce simple math and science concepts. Enjoy hours of fun!

GO TO: www.curiousgeorgebooks.com

Enter your secret password **LEARN**

A FROG'S LIFE

Many animals change body shapes over the course of their life cycles. Frogs are one kind. Can you think of any others?

Here are the main stages of a frog's life, out of order. Number them one to four in the proper order.

FROG
(12-16 WEEKS)

EGGS
(BEFORE HATCHING)

TADPOLE WITH LEGS
(6-9 WEEKS)

TADPOLE
(BIRTH-4 WEEKS)

Here are some: mosquitoes, butterflies, ladybugs, silkworms, mealworms, ants, cicadas

Curious George®

The Boat Show

**Adaptation by Kate O'Sullivan
Based on the TV series teleplay
written by Raye Lankford**

Houghton Mifflin Harcourt Publishing Company
Boston New York

For information about permission to reproduce selections from this book, write to Permissions, Houghton Mifflin Harcourt Publishing Company, 215 Park Avenue South, New York, New York 10003.

Library of Congress Cataloging-in-Publication Data is on file.

ISBN: 978-0-547-691107

Design by Afsoon Razavi

www.hmhbooks.com

Printed in China
LEO 10 9 8 7 6 5 4 3 2 1
4500292891

AGES	GRADES	GUIDED READING LEVEL	READING RECOVERY LEVEL	LEXILE ® LE
5-7	1-2	I	15-16	380L

It was a beautiful day and
George was curious.
He was curious about all the
boats on the river.

George liked one boat best of all.
It was carrying cars!
"That is a ferryboat," said the man
with the yellow hat.

George liked to boat watch but
he was eager to get to the lake.
If he was lucky, he might see
another ferryboat.

At the lake
there were lots of people.
They were watching the model
boat contest.
There were boats of all kinds.

Bill showed George his model
sailboat.
George thought it was wonderful.

"I saved a lot of
money to build this boat," Bill said.
"Will you keep it safe until the
contest?"

George was happy to help.
He held the boat very carefully.

He looked at the boat.
He looked at his toy cars.
George had an idea.

George made Bill's boat look just like a ferryboat.

Oh, no!
It sank.
What would Bill enter into the contest now?

George tried to make another
boat for Bill out of his toys.
It sank, too.
George saw that some of the toys
floated.
He had a better idea.

George looked at other boats
on the river.
He made plans to build a boat
from his floating toys.
Bill would be proud.

When Bill came back, he saw the
new boat.
"That is a great ferryboat!" Bill said.

Then George showed Bill what
had happened to the sailboat.

"Uh-oh!" Bill said.
"I forgot to shut the boat's windows.
I'll fix that.

Now water cannot get inside and
the boat will float.
Let's go enter our boats in the
contest!"

Everyone won a blue ribbon for
all their hard work—even George.

SHIPS AHOY!

Make a paper boat.

1. Take a sheet of paper and fold it in half.

2. Fold down the top corners.   3. Fold up the bottom flaps.   4. Fold into the center.

5. Fold up the bottom half of one side. Repeat on the other side.

6. Push sides in and pull center toward you.

7. Pull sides away from each other to make your boat!

Now test your boat and see if it floats.

TO THE TOP

Gather the household items listed below. Ask a grownup to fill up the bathroom tub or sink, and see if they float!

	Float	Sink	Did you guess correctly?
Margarine tub			
Pencil			
Egg carton			
Magnet			
Flower			
Wooden block			
Crayon			
Rubber ball			
Plastic spoon			
Metal spoon			
Challenge: Watermelon			